vegetable families

Stem vegetables

asparagus

fennel

celery

Pulses

chickpeas

peas

lentils

runner beans

green beans

sweetcorn (maize)

Leafy vegetables

red cabbage

spinach

lamb's lettuce

Brussels sprouts

lettuce

endives

dandelion

Root vegetables

carrots

beetroot

celeriac

turnips

radishes

Thanks to Alain Douineau and Sophie Deschamps,
Jardin des Plantes botanical garden, Paris

Translated by Polly Lawson
First published in French under the title *Ça pousse comment?*
© 2013, l'école des loisirs, Paris
English edition © Floris Books 2014

British Library CIP Data available
ISBN 978-178250-037-7

Printed in Poland

How Does My Garden Grow?

Gerda Muller

Floris Books

Hooray for summer!

Sophie lived in a large city. The vegetables she ate usually came from the supermarket at the end of her street.

One summer, Sophie went to stay with her grandparents in the countryside. She said goodbye to her family and her best friend Victor before catching the train. Her grandparents grew vegetables, and Sophie was looking forward to doing lots of fun things in the garden.

That evening, she slept in a little bedroom under the eaves of the house. In the morning, the birds and sunshine woke her – along with the delicious smell of the hot chocolate her grandma was making for breakfast.

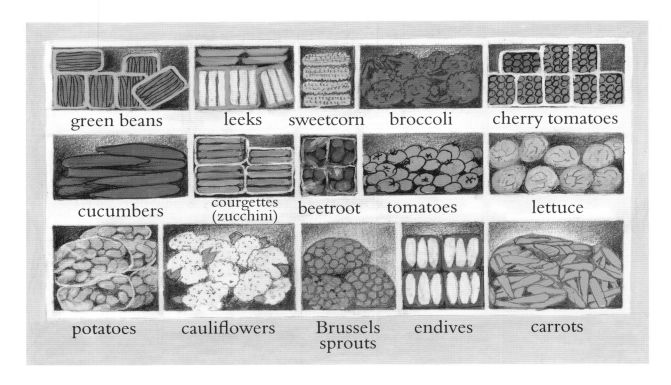

green beans   leeks   sweetcorn   broccoli   cherry tomatoes

cucumbers   courgettes (zucchini)   beetroot   tomatoes   lettuce

potatoes   cauliflowers   Brussels sprouts   endives   carrots

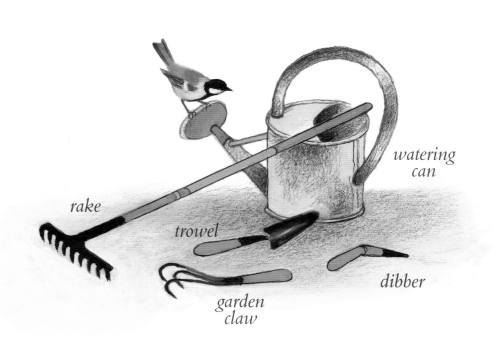

rake

trowel

watering can

garden claw

dibber

After breakfast, Grandad John took her out into the garden and gave her lots of tools, all just the right size.

"Oh, thank you!" said Sophie.

Grandad John showed Sophie a small patch of garden where she could grow her own vegetables. "Before sowing the seeds, you need to rake the ground."

"I'd like to sow carrots, radishes and lettuce," Sophie decided.

Grandad John gave her three seed packets and labels. Then he marked three rows with the handle of the rake, and placed a bucket of earth nearby.

Sophie wrote the names of the vegetables on the labels and stuck them into the ground. Next she carefully scattered the seeds along the rows. It wasn't easy! Finally she covered the rows with extra earth from the bucket, and watered them.

"Well done, my little gardener!" said Grandad John. "In a few weeks, you'll be able to crunch your very own radishes."

Better than candy

The next day, a little boy called Tom joined Sophie and Grandad John in the garden. Grandad John was carrying a basket full of straw.

"I've invited our young neighbour to help pick the peas," said Grandad John. "But first we need to mulch the onions, which means we spread straw around them. Let's go!"

Sophie and little Tom had a great time.

"What does the straw do?" asked Sophie.

"It keeps the earth damp and stops weeds from growing," explained Grandad John. "And as soon as you've finished, we can munch the freshest peas ever!"

He split open a pea pod and rolled peas into Sophie's hand. She closed her eyes and tasted one. "It's delicious!"

"They're really sweet," agreed little Tom. "Better than candy!"

The birds loved the fresh, raw peas too, but thankfully the cat was nearby, so they didn't steal too many.

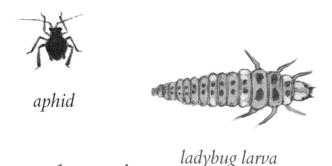

Grandad John liked ladybugs, because they eat aphids, which suck sap from plants and make them weaker.

aphid

ladybug larva

ladybug

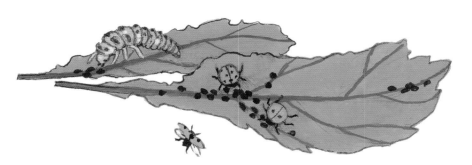

Ladybugs and their larva like eating aphids.

two pea pods, nine peas, one shallot, one onion, three radishes, three green beans

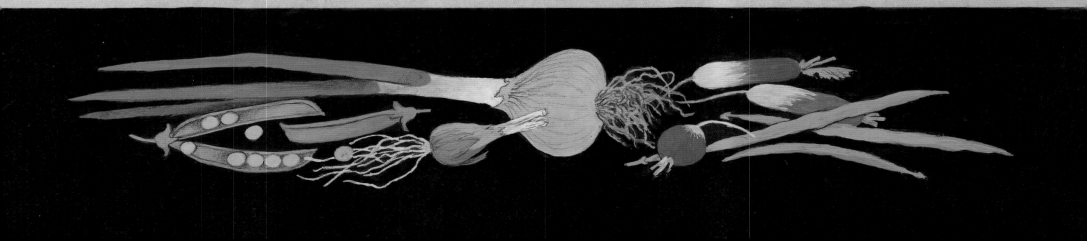

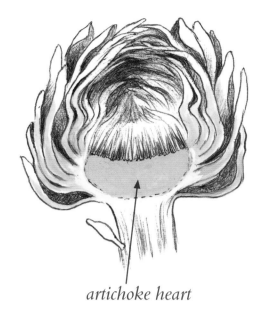

artichoke heart

cabbage white butterfly

The cabbage white caterpillar likes eating cabbage leaves.

Flowers for dinner

"What's for dinner tonight, Grandad John?"

"Flowers."

"Flowers? Yuck!" cried Sophie. "I'm much too hungry to eat flowers!"

"Well, come with me."

Grandad John showed Sophie a beautiful bush of tall artichoke stems.

"We need to cut the artichokes before they start to flower," he said. "We'll eat the hearts."

"I love artichoke hearts," said Sophie.

Next Grandad John cut a head of broccoli.

"With broccoli, we really are eating the flowers. They're delicious. But I'm going to put a net over them to stop the pigeons eating them. Look, the broccoli and cauliflowers are thirsty."

"I'll water them," said Sophie.

one cauliflower, one artichoke, one head of broccoli

Peas and bees

A path in the garden was overgrown with weeds. Grandma skilfully pulled them out with a hoe, and Sophie helped with her garden claw. While they were weeding, they sang songs. "Weeding is fun!" said Sophie.

Over in the cold frames, the lettuce seeds were growing into little plants, kept warm by the glass.

"It's time to transplant them into the main garden," said Grandad John, "so they've got room to grow bigger."

"I'll help," said Sophie. "I've got my dibber."

Sophie made equally spaced holes in the earth along Grandad John's neat rows, and carefully planted the baby lettuces. Finally, she watered the little plants.

That evening, Sophie and her grandma were strolling in the garden. They stopped and looked at the bees buzzing around the flowering pea plants.

"Bees are so important," said Grandma. "Without them, flowers wouldn't be pollinated and become pea pods, and there wouldn't be any peas."

"How does a flower turn into a pea pod?" asked Sophie.

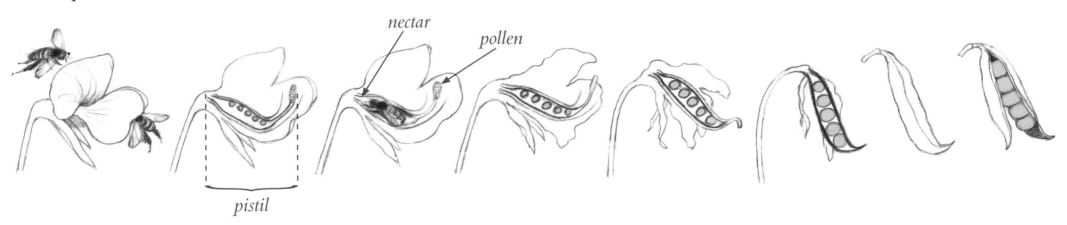

nectar

pollen

pistil

Grandma fetched a pencil and paper.

"Here's the flower... with tiny peas along its pistil, sweet nectar at its centre and a fine dust called pollen at the end of the pistil. When the bee goes into the flower to drink nectar, it gets covered in pollen, which it carries to the next flower it visits. The pollen rubs off onto the tiny peas in the next flower and makes them grow."

"Wow! Bees are amazing!" cried Sophie.

Digging up lunch

The next morning, Grandad John's back was aching, so he had to rest. Their neighbour Lucas came over to help dig up some potatoes. Each plant had lots of potatoes of different sizes clustered around the original seed potato, which was now black and shrivelled.

Sophie carefully dug up a lovely big carrot with her trowel.

"Well done!" said Lucas.

"I'm going to dig up some more for lunch," said Sophie. "Carrots are tasty."

"Can I have the carrot tops?" asked Lucas. "My rabbit loves the stalks and leaves."

The asparagus were also big enough to harvest and eat. What a treat!

If carrots aren't dug up in time, they will grow very tall and flower.

That evening, Lucas's rabbit enjoyed a crunchy dinner of carrot tops.

Garlic bulbs are made up of several cloves. If you plant a clove in the ground, it will grow into a new plant!

three asparagus, one carrot top, two carrots, one potato

Sunbathers

The days were getting very hot, so the plants were thirsty. Sophie watered the pumpkins, melons and cucumbers.

"Fancy a ride in my wheelbarrow-taxi?" said Grandad John. "Let's take a delivery next door to Lucas."

"Why are the pumpkins and melons on little platforms?" asked Sophie.

"So they don't get wet in the damp earth."

"It's funny that some vegetables grow under the ground and others above."

"Root vegetables like carrots and radishes grow underground. Fruits with seeds inside grow above; we often eat them raw in salads," Grandad John explained.

"So when I eat a tomato or cucumber, I'm eating a kind of fruit?"

"That's right."

two cucumbers, five gherkins, two pumpkins, one melon, three courgettes (zucchini)

Pipistrelles are very useful bats, because they eat insect pests. In the daytime, bats sleep upside down in caves or trees. Their babies catch a lift by clinging to their mothers' furry tummies.

Night-time secrets

One night, there was a full moon. Sophie was asleep, so she didn't see the bats swooping above the garden, and she didn't see the three field mice nibbling the vegetables.

But the cat saw them. "Mmm... delicious," it thought. "Dinner!"

The peppers were ripening in the warm greenhouse, and as they did, they changed colour: first green, then yellow, then red.

The next morning, Sophie asked, "Do plants keep growing at night-time?"

"No," said Grandma, who was chopping beetroot, "but they get stronger overnight, just like you when you're asleep."

"Can I make beetroot salad for lunch?" asked Sophie. "With a surprise..."

Sophie's beetroot salad: peel and cube the beetroot, add the same quantity of apple (the secret ingredient!), and season with salad dressing.

one turnip, one beetroot, one bulb of fennel, one pepper

Birds, beetles and broadforks

Because it was so hot, Sophie and Grandad John made a bird bath.

"I'll look after it," said Sophie.

The birds loved splashing around in their bath, so it needed a lot of cleaning!

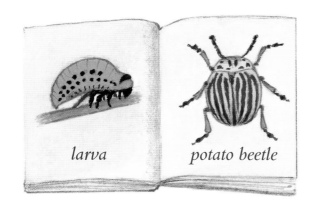

larva   *potato beetle*

Then disaster struck! A swarm of potato beetles, which eat the leaves of potato plants, invaded the local vegetable gardens. All the neighbours worked together to catch the insects.

Later that afternoon, when they had finished clearing the beetles, Lucas came over with a giant, two-handled broadfork.

"Watch, Sophie!" he said. "This broadfork is much gentler than a normal garden fork. I can use it to break up the earth without disturbing all the helpful creatures that live there."

Sophie invited Lucas and little Tom to a picnic on the lawn. They had radishes, tomato tart and juicy melon – all from the garden, of course.

"Oh no, it's starting to rain!" shouted Sophie.

But Grandad John smiled and sighed happily. "Finally, some rain for my thirsty garden."

They had to finish their picnic indoors.

If lettuce isn't picked in time, it will grow very tall and flower (this is called 'going to seed').

Vegetable peelings, tea leaves, coffee grains, dead leaves and weeds can go on the compost heap. They will be transformed into nutritious compost.

A windy night

That night, the wind was very strong. So strong that several tall maize stalks fell over, and some broke.

"Don't worry, Grandad John," said Sophie, "I can help."

"I'm so glad you're here," he replied. "We can earth up the fallen stalks together."

"Earth up?" asked Sophie.

"Yes, that's when we pile up earth around the base of the stems and firm it down; it helps to keep the stems upright."

Sophie gathered the dead leaves and Grandad John cut the broken stalks into little pieces.

"We'll put it all on the compost heap," he said.

one cob of corn, ten cherry tomatoes, one tomato, one plum tomato, two different lettuce leaves

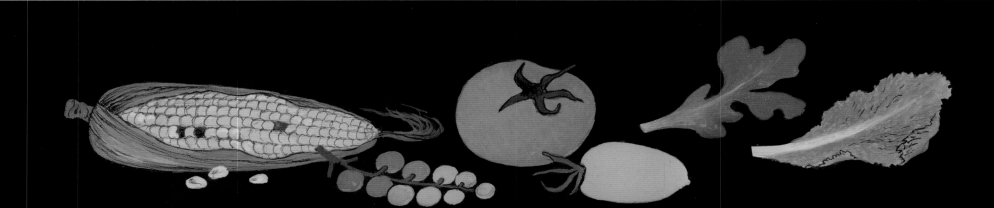

Market

Shed where endives
are grown

FRESH VEGETABLES

Off to market

When Grandad John had harvested lots of
vegetables, he put them in his red van and drove to
the local market. Sophie loved going with him.

"But where do the vegetables in the supermarket
come from?" asked Sophie.

"They come from the big fields you can see over
there. There are thousands of potatoes in one field.
They're harvested early in the morning, taken to

Giant water sprinkler

Max Potiron & Sons Preserves

ENTRANCE

OFFICE

DELIVERIES

Max Potiron & Sons

Co-operative Supermarket

town in lorries, and stacked into supermarket boxes. Other vegetables go to Mr Potiron's factory where they are preserved in jars."

"And what happens in that building over there?"

"That's where they grow endives. Endives grow in the cold and dark because light makes them go green and taste bitter," explained Grandad John.

"Brrr, I'm glad I don't have to work in there," said Sophie. "I like the sun too much!"

Autumn days

In September, Sophie went back to school in the city, but she soon visited her grandparents again. The vegetable garden looked very different.

Sophie helped her grandma cut Brussels sprouts. "They look funny," she said, "like little cabbages on a long stalk."

"That's because they're the buds of the cabbage plant," Grandma explained. "This evening, we'll eat them with some tasty sausages! Now, it's starting to get cold. Let's hang up a fat ball and seeds for the birds. All sorts of birds will come and peck at them; there are no insects to eat in winter, so they get very hungry."

"I'll climb up to hang it," offered Sophie.

Sophie noticed a strange-looking leek. "Grandma," she cried, "it's covered in red spots, as if it's got measles!"

"Oh dear," said Grandma. "It has rust disease. We'd better pull it up quickly."

Insects hibernate through the cold winter months. Grandad John made them a special hotel from a wooden box filled with hollow branches and twigs, facing the sun.

Gardeners love earthworms! They eat the earth and make it richer, and their little tunnels trap air in the ground.

A shy hedgehog was hiding under the red cabbages. It had spotted some fat, tasty slugs, which it would eat as soon as Sophie and her grandma left. Gardeners love hedgehogs because they eat slugs and snails.

two leeks, one green cabbage leaf, five Brussels sprouts, half a red cabbage

The Jerusalem artichoke flower is a cousin to the sunflower.

Wrap up warm!

It was a very cold night, but that didn't stop the gardeners from heading out the next day, wrapped up warm.

Grandad John used a fork to dig up Jerusalem artichokes, pulling hard on the stalks.

Sophie gathered some crunchy green lamb's lettuce, then replaced the plank of wood that had been protecting them. She was very proud of her mini salad plants.

A big celeriac root was keeping warm under its bed of straw. And the endives, which would soon poke their noses out of the earth, were still hidden underground.

Every three years, Grandad John dug fertiliser into the earth to add nutrients, so the vegetables would grow better. The fertiliser was made from straw mixed with horse manure. Grandad John didn't mind the smell, but Sophie held her nose... and ran away!

Moles can be very useful in a garden, because they eat little creatures that munch through vegetable roots and leaves.

A mole's favourite menu:

mole

snail

May beetle grub

slug

three Jerusalem artichokes, one endive, three pieces of lamb's lettuce, one celeriac root

A blanket of snow

There was lots to do in the vegetable garden before winter came, so Sophie came back one weekend to lend a hand.

They had to clean the stakes and canes and store them in the shed.

They had to pull up any dead stems and tomato plants, and burn them.

Grandad John had sown a special crop that would stay in the ground all winter. In the spring, he would plough it into the earth to make it richer. He called it a 'green cover crop'.

Now that Sophie and her grandparents had finished their jobs, the garden – covered in snow – could rest until spring.

Spot the tools in the shed

boots
broadfork
canes
clogs
fork
garland of onions
gloves
hoe
rafia
rake
secateurs
spade
trowel

Sophie's tools

dibber
garden claw
rake
trowel
watering can

Before she went home, Sophie tidied her tools in the shed and said goodbye to the neighbours. After a wonderful year, she felt sad to be leaving the vegetable garden, the village and especially her grandparents. But Grandad John had a surprise, to help Sophie feel better...

A city vegetable garden

Back at home, in the first days of spring sunshine, Sophie and her best friend Victor opened the present from her grandparents. What a lovely surprise! It was full of packets of vegetable and herb seeds.

"We can grow plants, just like in the country!" Sophie laughed.

Grandad John had drawn a picture of a sun on some packets, which meant: this plant needs sunlight. Victor's window faced south and got lots of sun, but Sophie's balcony had a mixture of sun and shade.

The two friends divided up the seeds. But what could they plant them in?

With their parents' help, they bought big pots and planters, bags of earth and canes. Once the seeds were sowed, they waited, watered regularly, and waited some more.

After a few weeks, the radishes appeared, and other vegetables and herbs followed. Sophie and Victor's friends came round to see and taste them – and decided *they* wanted to grow vegetables on their window sills as well.

Now Sophie had her very own garden!

Victor made an omelette from all the delicious herbs, and added edible flower petals to a salad. Scrumptious!

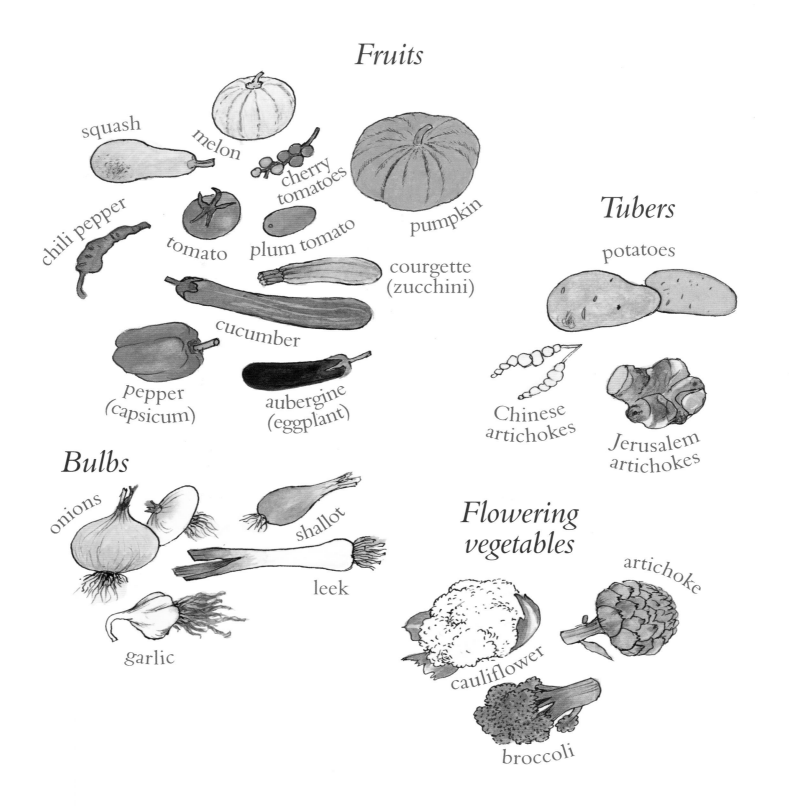

Fruits

squash

melon

cherry tomatoes

pumpkin

chili pepper

tomato

plum tomato

Tubers

potatoes

courgette (zucchini)

cucumber

Chinese artichokes

Jerusalem artichokes

pepper (capsicum)

aubergine (eggplant)

Bulbs

onions

shallot

Flowering vegetables

leek

artichoke

garlic

cauliflower

broccoli